The Adventures of Tom Wandermind

Synopsis

13-year-old Tom Wandermind takes you on his adventure around the world. Today, on his 13th birthday, his father purchased him a new bike. Not only was this bike amazing looking, but it had special powers that only Tom would discover. This new bike takes him on many quests and adventures. Will Tom be able to overcome the challenges he faces, and have fun on his new bike? Or will he experience the best journey he has ever been on?

Illustrated by Jason Rosado

For Serenity and Matteo. I love you

CONTENTS

FOREWORD

Do you feel exhausted after taking a flight of stairs in your building? Can you imagine what it would take to scale a mountain? Well, an 8-year-old Indian kid just finished climbing a 5,642-metre-high mountain and we are astonished. Ayaan Saboor Mendon, an Indian expat from Dubai has achieved a milestone which would be a distant dream for some of us.

A young mountaineer from Dubai who is eight years old has reached the summit of Europe. Along with his mother Vani Mendon and father Saboor Ahmad, Indian-born **Ayaan Saboor Mendon** scaled Mount Elbrus.

After building a target of eight days, the young hiker, last month, completed the 5,642-meter-high peak in just five days. The 8-year-old Indian kid had already scaled Mount

Kilimanjaro in Tanzania and Mount Kosciuszko in Australia, so this was not his first summit.

Additionally, he has participated in Tough Mudder and Spartan races. His ambitions to conquer mountains are also growing.

The child engages in rigorous training. It includes treadmill jogging, walking tied with big weights, sledge push workouts, and hurdle course training. That seems a lot for an 8-year-old kid but that's what makes him a mountaineer at such a young age.

The young man told the National during an interview that there was often no visibility due to dense clouds. While trailing with his parents he needed to be careful of incoming thunderstorms. He continued by saying that his objective for this year was to summit three of the world's tallest mountains in less than a year. Ayaan intends to climb

Argentina's 6,961-metre-tall Mount Aconcagua in December 2023.

Before that, he will climb Island Peak (Imja Tse) in Nepal in October 2023. Further, he plans Mentok Kangri II in Ladakh, India, towards the end of July 2023. Once he becomes 12 years old, his ultimate objective is to climb Mount Everest, the tallest mountain in the world.

This young man seems full of ambition and fascination for the mountains. Can you imagine yourself reaching a summit someday?

ABOUT THE AUTHOR

Michael Walker-Thomas, Born March 2, 1988, is an Educator, Author, Poet and Owner. He found his love for writing at a young age by reading Encyclopedia Brown, Magic School Bus and Goosebumps. Michael's writing influences are W.E.B. Du Bois, Carter G. Woodson, Maya Angelou and James Baldwin. Michael also loves the movies Finding Forrester, He Got Game, Super 8 and Inception as writing inspirations. He is the author of several books, including A Boy With a Dream, Sibling Strong, Chess Moves 1 and 2, The Voices You May Not Hear and The Voices You May Not Hear:The Lost Pages. His new book "God A:M and God P:M" is out now! His Book Chess Moves is sold worldwide and in over 40 Countries.

You can follow him on Instagram @bookofmichael

CHAPTER I

The Wish

There once was a boy named Tom, whose quest took him far and wide. Tom was a normal boy, someone with a large mind. Tom wanted to travel the world, but his parents didn't travel much. When Tom was younger, he created a list of places he wanted to travel to, Europe, North America, South America, Africa, and many more. Today is his birthday. Today, Tom is hoping for lots of gifts. His dad told him that when he comes home from school, he has a gift waiting for him. Tom was excited. Tom went to school that morning smiling ear to ear. The class sang happy birthday, he had cupcakes from his teacher, he received many high fives, and he was a TEENAGER. Being a teenager meant a lot to Tom. Tom knew this was going to be a big year. The good for Tom was to travel, and by travel, I mean TRAVEL. All those places, all the food, all the sights. Traveler Tom was ready. There was only one problem. Tom didn't have the money. Tom thought about his allowance money, selling items, or starting a Gofundme. Tom immediately felt sad, but overall, he had a fun day at school.

Tom rushed home and put his backpack down. He looked and shouted for his dad, but he was not home yet. His mother explained to him that his dad was picking up a few things after work. Tom began to watch TV. He loved cartoons, sports and travel shows. Toms favorite cartoon is Hey Arnold!, his favorite sport is Baseball, and his favorite travel show is Somebody Feed Phil. He could watch those for hours! Tom heard the door open, it was his dad. Tom gave him a hug and a hand slap. His dad had a cake, a card, and some flowers for his mom. He then asked Tom to come outside. Tom walked outside and he saw his gift. A BLUE SHINY BIKE. This bike looked amazing. This bike was shiny. This was the best, nicest, and coolest bike Tom had ever seen. The tires were new, the chain shiny, pegs on the back, and best of all, it had grips on the handles. Tom runs towards the shiny blue bike and gets on it. He feels like he is on top of the world! Tom is happy, today is a great day. Tom is overfilled with joy.

Tom's dad told him the bike was something special. He said when he went to the store, the owner of the shop kept questioning and asking him if he wanted this bike. Tom's dad told him that once he saw the bike, he knew it would be perfect for him. Tom then took the bike for a ride around the neighborhood, with his mom and dad by his side. He learned how to ride a bike when he was 5 years old. Tom learned a lot of things, swimming, baseball, basketball, football, piano, but the best of all of these was riding a bicycle. Once he got on this bike, it made him feel like he was on top of the world. After Tom had ridden his bike, he headed in for dinner. His mom made him his favorite food, Lasagna, and all three of them then ate cake. His mom asked him to make a wish before they ate the cake. Tom did. A

special day, for a special boy, Tom was tired.

CHAPTER 2

Africa

Tom went upstairs and watched TV in his room for hours, well it felt like hours. His TV started to black out and then he got up. He went to go ask his parents for help with the TV, but his door would not open. He then yelled for his parents, but they did not come. Tom was trapped. Tom then looked outside and saw the sun and a desert. This desert was called the Sahara Desert. Tom yelled some more, but no one could hear him. He then looked outside again. There, on the sand, was one thing. Tom kept rubbing his eyes, but he wasn't sleeping. That one thing on the sand, was his brand new Blue Shiny Bike.....

Tom jumped out the window and saw many Ergs, which are sand dunes. They looked deep, deep enough to trap you. Tom said no way to those. Tom looked amazed at this place.

From the Regs, to the Hamadas, it was amazing. It was so hot outside, so Tom hopped on his new bike and went to go find some water. In the distance, Tom saw mountains and trees. This place was beautiful, like a movie. Many grasslands covered this place, and Tom was still in awe. Tom approached a store and went inside. He asked the man at the register for water and the man said the water is in the back. Tom then asked him a question. He asked the man where he was. The man said Africa. Tom shouted AFRICA! then fainted.

After Tom awoke, the man opened the water bottle and Tom drunk it. The man then asked Tom where his parents where, but Tom hopped on his bike and left. Africa, a beautiful place that Tom has never been to. Tom remembered what he wished, and then it hit him. The Blue Shiny Bike got him here. Tom was afraid he was going to run into some animals like Lions, Zebras, Hyenas, and Giraffes. He did not see any yet. Then suddenly, a lion comes racing toward Tom. Tom gets scared and starts to ride away, but the lion yells stop. Tom couldn't believe that the lion could speak. The lion comes towards Tom and welcomes him. He explains to Tom that he can speak, and not to be afraid of him. The lion then explains to him that Africa is a beautiful place. The lion tells Tom about the land, the water, and the food. Tom became excited and was smiling ear to ear. The lion explains to Tom that even though Africa is nice, he says don't get stuck here. Tom wonders what he means. Tom then travels to the Swahili Coast. This place was a beautiful, sandy area. Tom saw the Indian Ocean and lots of trees. Then Tom went to the Congo River and its Rainforest. Tom has never been to the rainforest.

His parents once took him to the aquarium and the zoo. That is as close as he got to seeing these types of things. There were so many birds there that Tom had to duck his head every time one flew passed him. He then saw amazing looking butterflies; they were all types of colors. Tom wanted to go to the lake next, so he went. He went to the Great Lakes. He saw many fish, and more animals. He rested there for what seemed like an hour. He then rode his bike to this mountain. The mountain was huge. Tom was so amazed that he wanted to fly his bike up the mountain. This mountain was Kilimanjaro, the almost 20,000 feet (about 6.1 km) high monster.

Tom began to fly up the mountain, soaring through the clouds and the air. Tom got to the top of the mountain and saw another person. He can't make out this figure, and then he could. It was the lion. The lion says Tom is staying here. Tom gets scared. He explains to him that he just turned 13, he needs to get back home, and he misses his friends. The lion disagrees. He explains to Tom that the bike he is riding belongs to him and to get off. The lions then chased Tom around the mountain, then Tom finally hoped on his bike, and flew away. Tom was relieved to get away from the lion. All he remembers the lion saying was to not get stuck here.

Tom is finally on to his next adventure.

CHAPTER 3

Europe

Tom then arrives at this amazing looking place. He sees lots of people and places to shop. He sees water, smells food, and hears other languages. Tom only knows one language. He then rides his bike through this place, and the people look at him while he rides. Tom flies over the Peninsulas. He has never seen anything so unique. The borders of these peninsulas were the Atlantic, the Artic, the Mediterranean, and the Caspian. He then flew to the Alpine Mountain. He did not stay long, he thought that lion would be up there. He loved looking at mountains, it was a favorite sight to see. Tom then flew over the sea. He looked down at the water and seen so many amazing animals. From a distance, he saw this place across the water, it was amazing looking as well.

This place was called Iceland. He had to fly a long way on his bike, but it was worth it. This place had power plants, mountains, lots of grass, and waterfalls. Tom stayed there for what seemed like a few hours. He ate food from one of the shops. He then went back across the water to Italy. He passed by those amazing looking seas again. He traveled down to the beach and saw many people again. Tom spoke to the locals and tourists. Tom then gets some lemonade and walks his bike to the shops. A local told Tom not to travel to the volcanoes, they could be dangerous. Tom asks the local if he ever heard of a talking lion, but the local was confused.

Tom toured Rome, Venice, and Florence. He had a great time. The last thing he did was see a painting by Leonardo da Vinci, he was amazed. Tom then left for Paris, and of course he had to have some Pizza in his hand as he flew across the city. He landed next to the Eiffel Tower. He saw this huge structure so many times on TV, and in movies.

Tom flew around it and waved to the people. The people waved back at Tom. He then went to a bridge with locks on it and read most of the names. He thought the bridge was the coolest thing in the world. Tom then ventured around the city and saw so many beautiful buildings. He saw the Hotel des Invalides, Arc de Triomphe, and many museums. Tom then became tired, and he then let his new Blue Shiny Bike fly him to his next destination. Tom was so glad that he did not see the lion again.

CHAPTER 4

North America

Tom then was on top of this large building. The building looked different than what he had seen before. This building was the CN Tower. Tom was in Toronto. Once again, Tom saw so many tall buildings and huge bodies of water. The city was very busy as well. The people were walking fast, and Tom flew down to be with the people. He then saw some parks and decided to relax there. It was a great day for Tom to be at the park, the locals told him he picked a great time to be there. Tom once again heard many languages and smelled great food.

Tom then hopped on his bike and flew down to another place. This place was not too far away. This place had the most people walking around that he ever saw. He saw lights everywhere, and bridges with cars going back and forth. This place was New York City. The city that never sleeps.

Tom went to Times Square first. This place had many stores, characters, music, and people talking and walking. This place was loud. Tom saw many others with bikes, but not as nice as his. Those people had food on their bikes, and they had uniforms on. Tom then went to the bridges. He saw the Brooklyn Bridge, The George Washington Bridge, The Manhattan Bridge, and many more. He then saw people playing basketball next to one of the bridges, and he sat and watched. Tom found it fascinating that the people were playing next to the water and a bridge. It was different than a hoop in a driveway or playing at a gym. Tom then spoke to some locals, and they told him to go to the giant lady statue. Tom rode his bike to the Statue of Liberty. This Statue was amazing to look at, and many people were taking pictures in front of it. Tom then hopped on his bike and flew away. He traveled for a time to a place that he had never been to. Tom saw land, then water, then land, then water. This place was called Florida. The Sunchine State.

Tom heard of Disney World, but he has never been. He then stumbled upon an ice cream place. Tom walked in with his bike and got some ice cream. He asked the worker if they could tell him where he was. The worker said Miami. Tom then asked him where Disney was. The worker said a few hours away. Tom left and saw many palm trees, nice cars, and many bridges once again. He rode his bike around for a while and visited the beaches. He once again heard many languages and seen many shops. This place was very nice, but Tom asked for directions to Disney. Tom flew away and headed towards it.

Tom then made it towards Disney World. He visited Hollywood Studios, Magic Kingdom, Animal Kingdom, and other parks. He then saw a lion. He was not sure if this was the same lion, or like characters that he saw in New

York. The lion did not notice him, as Tom hid behind a few trees with his bike. He then went on a few more rides and ate cotton candy, The lion was still there. Tom was getting really scared, as he did not think about the lion for a long time. Tom was ready to go. Tom got on his bike and flew away. Tom thought to himself that there's no way that the lion would be in North America. Tom wanted to get away fast, and in a hurry, far far away.

Tom landed his Blue Shiny Bike in California. Tom visited San Diego, Los Angeles, and finally San Francisco. Before arriving, when he was flying, Tom saw Yellowstone National Park. Tom was amazed. He loved the city he was in. He saw the Golden Gate Bridge, ate some food, and went up and down the city streets. He never saw streets that looked like this. These streets were on hills and they were very bumpy. He spoke to a tourist that was from a place in Pennsylvania, that had streets like this, but he had never seen anything like this before. In school, he read about the gold being here, the banks and the businesses, but seeing it firsthand was a sight to see. He seen many people that looked different, and that was great to see. Tom thought to himself how different it was, that even though everyone looked different, they all got along with each other. Tom then went to get something to eat, he ate Chinese food. The owner told him that the fortune cookie was invented in San Francisco. Tom then rode his bike to the streets, he wanted to ride the trolley before he left. He loved looking at the city and the many buildings. He then looked at the back of the trolley and saw someone running towards him.

IT WAS THE LION!! "I GOT YOU" the lion said.

Tom hopped on his bike and jumped out of the trolley. The lion followed him from the ground and was yelling to get off the bike. Tom kept shouting NO. The lion said he saw Tom at Disney World and in Toronto, but he could not get to him. Tom told the lion to leave him alone. The lion told

Tom that he would get his bike back and have him trapped here forever. Tom started panicking and flew into the sky.

Tom then landed on another Mountain. No buildings, no people, no food, no bridges. It was him, and the Rocky Mountains. Tom thought about his parents, his friends, his school. Tom missed home, but he loved traveling too. He knew that he dreamed of travelling, and this was what he wanted. He had to keep going and to not be afraid of the lion. The mountain he was on was called Elbert, and it was about 15,000 feet (about half the height of Mount Everest) high. These mountains are 80 million to 55 million years old. He remembered reading about Francisco Coronado, the first person to walk these mountains. Tom then flew down to the sand dunes and to the National Parks. Tom wandered around, and then he wondered where he would go next.

CHAPTER 5

South America

Tom then flew his bike and went down towards a forest. This forest was surrounded by mountains and water. He seen many animals in this forest. Monkeys, sloths, snakes, iguanas, and more. He also saw parrots, toucans, and parakeets. The birds stared at him flying and began to fly with him. One of the birds said hello, and another welcomed him. Tom asked the bird about this place and where he was at. The bird told Tom he was in South America. Tom was mesmerized by the landscapes, mountains, and trees. Tom then flew down to the second longest river in the world, The Amazon River. He flew his bike all over the water and laughed and smiled. Tom was so happy, and as much as he missed home, he was having the time of his life. The birds told him about the lungs of the earth, which was the rainforest.

Tom then started to get hungry. He went to the city and ordered some food. The locals told him the best thing to order was Feijoada. He ordered it, and then enjoyed this yummy sensation. Tom then asked for some chocolate and the owner of the shop gave him some Brigadeiro.

The owner asked Tom if his parents drank coffee, and Tom said yes. The owner told Tom that Brazil is the biggest coffee producer in the world.

He went on to explain that 300,000 coffee plantations are all over the land of Brazil. Tom said he sees all the soccer jerseys, and the owner explained to him how big soccer was there. Tom said he watches soccer sometimes. Tom then asked him where the most beautiful place was to see. The owner told Tom to go to the Iguacu National Park. He then asked Tom how he was going to get there, Tom told him he was going to fly. The owner didn't believe him.

Tom then hopped on his bike and flew away. The owner of the shop waved at Tom in disbelief, as he flew away. Tom flew to the National Park, and he was stunned. He had never seen so many waterfalls. There were over 2,000 plants here. Tom flew over many plants, and he kept seeing different ones. Tom also saw many toucans, he loved looking at these birds. He stayed here for some time and then left. He headed towards a huge statue. No, this wasn't the Statue of Liberty, this was Christ the Redeemer. The figure was fascinating to see. This was the best, most amazing, most fulfilling statue he had ever seen. The statue had its arms out, and Christ was looking down. The statue was 98 feet tall and weighed 65 metric tons. The arms stood 28 meters wide. Tom didn't have to walk the 200 steps like the other tourists, but he was happy he saw it. Tom was happy about his time in South

America. Tom wondered where he would travel next. He

hopped on his bike and took off.

CHAPTER 6

Australia

Tom flew to what seemed like a long way. He was tired, but he wasn't sleepy. Tom saw the water once again, but this time it took him forever to get over the water. He then saw this large place, the land covered what seemed like most of the ocean. His shiny blue bike flew him down to this place. Thia place was large. He saw people swimming, surfing, sailing, playing sports, and relaxing. Tom thought to himself how amazing this place looked. Tom then seen a large herd of animals. Tom had never seen one of these animals before in person. The animal was a Kangaroo. The Kangaroo came up to Tom, the other Kangaroos all stopped and looked at him. Welcome to Australia, the Kangaroo said.

The Kangaroo explained to Tom that his home has many parks, and he has other friends, like the Kaola Bear. He then scares Tom by telling him about the most dangerous animal on the planet. He tells Tom to take a guess. Tom guesses Shark, Whale, and Lion. The Kangaroo says no it is a spider. He explains to Tom that it is a funnel web spider, and they are poisonous. He tells Tom to stay away if you see one. He also tells Tom that there are also 20 types of venomous snakes, including the taipan, which attacks without warning and bites repeatedly, killing its victim in minutes. Tom asks him about rainforest because he has seen some before. He explains to Tom that there are several types of rain forests in Australia. Tropical rain forests, mainly found in the northeast, are the richest in plant and animal species. Subtropical rain forests are found near the mid-eastern coast, and broadleaf rain forests grow in the southeast and on the island of Tasmania. Tom continues to ride his bike around, while the Kangaroo hops next to him. The Kangaroo finally tells him to have fun. Tom sees so many different types of food. He sees wheat, beef, fruits, and berries. He also smells the other food.

Tom talks to some locals, and they tell him that he is on the oldest continent. The local also gives Tom some food and asks about his bike. Tom explains to her that it is his birthday present. Tom loves his bike and says he wants to ride it every day. He told the local that he wants to have some fun. She then told him about a magical park. She tells Tom about this place called Dreamworld on the gold coast. She said it is amazing. Tom flies his bike to this place. It takes him some time to get there, but he finally arrives.

Dreamworld looks amazing. It has rides, food, games, and people, LOTS OF PEOPLE. First, Tom gets on a few rides. He rides The Claw, Sky Voyager, The Giant Drop, and more. He was afraid of Steel Taipan, but he faced his fears and got on the ride. The whole time on the ride he felt like he was going to throw up, but he didn't. He loved it. Then Tom became hungry, and he went to get food. He ordered so much. He ordered five hot dogs, chicken, and cotton candy.

Tom then became tired. He went over to a water park with his bike. He sat back and started to realize how much fun he was having. Australia was amazing.

CHAPTER 7

Asia

Tom then wakes up and his bike tires are still spinning as he looks down. He is on a road, and then he lifts his head up. He is in the middle of a parade. This parade has many characters, people, and everyone is cheering. Welcome Tom, welcome! Everyone is shouting at him.

Welcome to the largest Continent. Tom remembers someone else told him that. Tom tells them that he knows he is in Australia, but they said no. Welcome to Asia.

Hey Tom, did you know that in China alone, we have as many people that live here compared to Australia, New Zealand, North America, South America and Western Europe combined? The local man explains to him these facts. He then continues. Our largest country is Russia, our largest city is Tokyo, our smallest country is Maldives. Hey Tom, let's go to the Yangtze River and I will tell you more. Tom then flies away with the local man. He continues to tell Tom more and more about Asia. Tom told him he loves mountains, and that he would love to see Mt Everest. They fly up to the mountain, and the tour continues. The local then tells Tom to enjoy Asia, and then he flies away. Tom wanted to do something different, he wanted to have others fly with him, using his pegs. He wanted to learn more about this large place. He then flew around and wanted to gain more knowledge. Each time he picked someone up he learned more.

First, he started with a tourist named Matthew.

"There are many ethnic groups in Asia. This is a huge continent, where vastly different cultures are practiced. In India and China, the most populous countries in Asia, there are many different ethnic groups all with their own distinct language and culture."

Next to speak was David."

"India is not only the second most populous country in Asia, but it has also the largest number of poor people and child laborers. One in four Indians cannot read or write. Then there are the Arabs, the Russians, Koreans, Japanese, Indians, Indonesians and so many more different cultural groups. There are also vast differences in living standards and poverty. In South-East Asia, most people live in rural areas outside the big cities which are underdeveloped."

Tom loved India. It was beautiful. He loved a place called Indore, it was amazing. He heard many stories about that place. They said many amazing people came from there.

Next to speak was John.

"However, Tom, there is also the tiny country of Singapore which is one of the richest, most modern and influential cities in the world. Singapore is a city state and leading country in modern technology and innovation and a major financial center."

Next to speak was Peter. They flew over The Great Wall of China. Which was amazing to see for Tom. Tom saw his favorite statue, which was in Brazil, but this wall was even bigger. Peter also showed him the Grand Palace in Thailand, the Taj Mahal, and the Water Temple in Bali. "Hey Tom, China has the most cities that houze more than 1 million inhabitants, there are 160 of such big cities in China! In comparison, inthe USA there are only 10 cities with more than 1 million inhabitants."

The last speaker was David.

"Hey Tom, in Asia, there are monkeys, tigers, Asian elephants and many other animals. Due to the different climates, we have snow leopards and polar bears in the north, and tropical species such as the Komodo dragons in the South. On some Indonesian islands, there are the largest living lizards, the Komodo dragons, which can eat very large animals such as a whole buffalo!"

"Tom, did you know that the Asian elephants are smaller than African elephants?"

Tom was finally hungry, and he ate some curry, fish, and some beef. He loved it so much. David then tells Tom one last thing. "Live your life to the fullest Tom and have fun. Give your all to what you love, then you will be happy." Tom said thank you and flew away. Tom learned so many facts today. Tom flew into the air with joy.

CHAPTER 8

Home

Tom was all smiles, he was absolutely having the time of his life, but he missed his home, his parents, and his friends. His journey was great. Tom then saw the Lion. The lion was chasing after him and would not stop. The lion jumped and ran, then jumped and ran. He was trying to

get his bike back. Tom told him that this bike was not his. "Lion, please stop, my father gave me this bike. It is mine." The lion explained to Tom that he would trap him here, and that it was his bike. Tom then rode faster, and the bike began to fly higher, and ride faster and faster. His new bike then did something it never did before, it circled around the lion and tied him up. The lion was now trapped. Tom got away. Tom then began to dose off, and his head fell on his handlebars. Tom visited all seven continents, he met so many amazing people, he ate great food, he loved sitting on the mountains, and more. Tom, most of all, enjoyed his new Shiny Blue Bike that his father gave him. His bike saved him.

In life, we must love the good times. In life, we must love the memories. In life, we must love the ones who help us. Tom finally woke up. His father and mother by his bedside shaking him. They said he fell off his bike and was feeling sick. His parents asked if he was feeling better. Tom said yes with a big smile. Tom told his father thank you for the bike. He told his mother thank you for a great birthday. Tom, in his mind, didn't fall off his bike. Tom had an adventure and had the time of his life.

AFTERWORD

Top 10 Reasons to Travel the World

- **New Experiences.**

- **Lasting Memories.**

- **Family Bonding.**

- **Trips are fun.**

- **We Don't Have Them Forever.**

- **Introductions to New Cultures and Ways of Living.**

- **Teach Experiences Over Possessions.**

- **New Opportunities for Responsibility.**

- **Travel Helps Break the Technology Addiction.**

- **Show Them It's Possible.**

"Travel because it makes you realize how much you haven't seen, how much you are not going to see, and how much you still need to see."

"The biggest adventure you can ever take is to live the life of your dreams."

— **Oprah Winfrey**